# Peter
# and the
# Wolf

Based on the story by Serge Prokofieff
Retold by Diane Redmond
Illustrated by John Bendall-Brunello

Collins

# CHARACTERS

The composer, Serge Prokofieff, wrote this as a musical story. In his story only the narrator uses words to speak. The other characters "speak" through musical instruments and each has its own tune.

Peter

Narrator

Grandfather

Hunter

Bird

Duck

Cat

Wolf

# SCENE 1. PETER'S COTTAGE

**NARRATOR:** Peter lived with his grandfather in a small cottage in the middle of a forest. In front of the cottage lay a big, green meadow.

**GRANDFATHER:** Don't play in the meadow, Peter. There's a wolf out there waiting to gobble you up.

**PETER:** *(crossly)* Humph! Who's afraid of the big, bad wolf? NOT ME! I'm going into the meadow – it's my *favourite* place to play.

3

# SCENE 2. THE MEADOW

**NARRATOR:** Peter ran into the meadow and met his friend, Bird.

**BIRD:** Tweet! Hello, Peter. Have you come to play with me?

**PETER:** *(bravely)* No. I'm going into the wood to catch the big, bad wolf.

*(A duck comes waddling into the meadow.)*

**DUCK:** Quack! Quack!
Don't go into the wood, Peter.
Come and have a swim with me.

**NARRATOR:** Duck waddled into the water and started to splash about. Bird thought she looked very funny and laughed at her.

**BIRD:** TWEET! What kind of bird are you if you can't fly?

**DUCK:** Quack! Quack! What kind of bird are you if you can't swim?

**BIRD:** TWEET! TWEET!

**DUCK:** QUACK! QUACK!

**NARRATOR:** Bird and Duck were arguing so much, they didn't see Cat come creeping up. Cat pounced at Bird …

**CAT:** Grrr! MIAOW!

**NARRATOR:** … but Bird flew up into the branches of a tall tree.

**BIRD:** Nah, nah, nah-nah, nah! You can't catch me.

**CAT:** (*crossly*) I don't care. I'll eat Duck instead.

**PETER:** Don't be silly. Duck's in the middle of the pond and you can't swim.

**CAT:** Miaow! Well, I'll climb the tree and get Bird.
*(Cat stares at Bird at the top of the tree.)*

**PETER:** *(laughing)* By the time you get up there, Bird will have flown away.

**CAT:** Miaow! I'll get you later.

**NARRATOR:** Suddenly Grandfather ran into the meadow, waving his arms. He looked very cross.

**GRANDFATHER:** *(angrily)* Peter! I told you *not* to play in the meadow. It's a dangerous place!

**PETER:** *(grumpily)* But Grandfather, I'm looking for the big, bad wolf.

**GRANDFATHER:** That's enough! Go straight to your room and stay there!

## SCENE 3. THE EDGE OF THE FOREST

**NARRATOR:** As soon as Peter and Grandfather had gone, a big, grey wolf came creeping out of the forest.

**WOLF:** Ha ha ha! Peter's gone. Now I can catch my dinner! (*The wolf creeps up on Cat.*)

**NARRATOR:** When Cat saw the wolf she jumped up into the tree.

**CAT:** MIAOW! MIAOOOOW!

**NARRATOR:** The wolf ran over to the pond. Duck saw the wolf, so she waddled out of the pond and tried to run away through the forest.

**DUCK:** QUACK! QUACK!

**WOLF:** Yummy! Duck dinner for me!

*(Duck runs away from the wolf, but he catches up with her.)*

**DUCK:** *(panting for breath)* Ah … ah … ah! I can't run any faster.

**NARRATOR:** The wicked wolf snapped hold of Duck's tail ... and with one big gulp, he swallowed her up.

**WOLF:** GULP! Slurp! Slobber!

**NARRATOR:** High up in the tree, Cat and Bird looked down at the wolf. The wolf looked up at them.

**WOLF:** (*licking his lips*) Yoo-hoo! I'm coming to get you, too.

**NARRATOR:** But Peter had seen everything. He climbed out of his bedroom window and ran back to the forest, carrying a strong rope.

**PETER:** (*whispering to himself*) I'm going to teach that wicked wolf a lesson.

*(Peter scrambles up the tree where Bird and Cat are sitting.)*

**PETER:** *(in a low voice)* Bird, go and fly around the wolf's head.

**BIRD:** TWEEET! No, he'll eat me.

**PETER:** Trust me! You must fly around the wolf, till he's sick and dizzy. And keep him near the bottom of the tree!

*(Bird flies round and round the wolf's head.)*

**BIRD:** WHEEEEEEE!

**WOLF:** OI! Silly Bird. Go away. You're making me dizzy.

*(Peter makes a lasso out of the rope, and dangles it down until it slips over the wolf's tail.)*

**NARRATOR:** The wolf didn't see Peter … but he felt the lasso when it was pulled tight round his tail.

17

**WOLF:** OWW! What's that! Get off my tail!

*(Peter ties the end of the rope round the thick branch he and Cat are sitting on – still high in the tree.)*

**PETER:** Ha ha! I've got you, you big, bad wolf.

**NARRATOR:** Just as Peter had tied up the wolf, a hunter came out of the forest and pointed his gun at Bird up in the tree.

**PETER:** Don't shoot! Bird and I have caught the big, bad wolf.

**HUNTER:** Amazing! Let's take him to the zoo.

# SCENE 4. THE ZOO

**NARRATOR:** Peter led the way to the zoo, followed by the hunter with the wolf. Grandfather went too, with Cat. Overhead, Bird chirped merrily.

20

**GRANDFATHER:** You're a brave boy, Peter. I'm not cross with you any more.

**BIRD:** Tweet, tweet. Peter is the bravest boy in the world.

**NARRATOR:** But what about Duck? If you listen very carefully, you'll hear Duck quacking inside the wolf. The wolf, in his hurry to eat her, had swallowed her whole.

**DUCK:** (*very quietly*) QUACK! QUACK! QUACK!

QUACK!

# WANTED

Someone to capture the big, bad wolf

**Must** be able to talk to animals

**Mustn't** be afraid of dark forests

**Must** be clever, quick and quite strong

**Must** be able to make a lasso
from a rope

**Must** be able to climb trees

**Don't** apply if you're scared
of wolves

**Don't** apply if you aren't
brave and clever

**Do** apply if your name is Peter

**Write to:**
**Hunter's Lodge, The Forest**

# Ideas for guided reading

**Learning objectives:** adopt appropriate roles in small or large groups; present traditional stories for members of the class; consider how mood and atmosphere are created; explain organisational features of texts; engage with books through exploring and enacting interpretations

**Curriculum links:** Music: Exploring sounds

**Interest words:** playscript, composer, instruments, scene, narrator, meadow, lasso

**Resources:** musical instruments; musical version of *Peter and the Wolf*

**Word count:** 870

## Getting started

- Ask the children if they know the story of *Peter and the Wolf.* Discuss what they know about wolves in stories.

- Read the front cover and blurb together. Discuss who the characters in this playscript might be.

- Turn to p2 and read the introduction to the children. Discuss the characters and check the children understand what a narrator does.

- Look at the instruments next to each character. (Peter: violin, Grandfather: bassoon, Hunter: timpani, Bird: flute, Duck: oboe, Wolf: French horn, Cat: clarinet). Discuss what sorts of sounds the instruments might make in the original musical score. What does this tell us about the characters?

## Reading and responding

- Discuss and agree who will read each role in the playscript (*the roles are divided between 6 readers and colour coded accordingly.*)

- Model how to read from the playscript. Draw their attention to the stage directions in brackets. Emphasise using a clear, audible voice and expression.